Nathan's Balloon Adventure

Lulu Delacre

SCHOLASTIC
HARDCOVER

SCHOLASTIC INC./New York

To Javi, with love

A LUCAS • EVANS BOOK

Library of Congress Cataloging-in-Publication Data
Delacre, Lulu.
Nathan's balloon adventure / by Lulu Delacre.   p.   cm.
Summary: Not a very welcome passenger, Nathan the elephant saves the day and makes a
friend when the hot air balloon carrying him and two mice runs out of fuel.
ISBN 0-590-44976-1
[1. Hot air balloons—Fiction.   2. Balloon ascensions—Fiction.   3. Elephants—Fiction.
4. Mice—Fiction.]   I. Title.
PZ7.D3696Nar   1991   [E]—dc20   90-26447   CIP   AC

12   10   9   8   7   6   5   4   3   2   1   1   2   3   4   5   6/9

Printed in the U.S.A.   36

First Scholastic printing, September 1991

For *Nathan's Balloon Adventure* I've used Windsor and Newton watercolors over
a smooth, French watercolor paper. My brushes range from 000 to number 6.
I use the smallest ones most often, since I delight in the tiniest of detail.
Everything in the book is watercolor except for Nathan himself. To make him
stand out, I use a different technique. I use prismacolor color pencils sharpened
to the maximum, and work very softly over the paper. To my eyes, this makes
him friendlier, warmer.

The air was still....

Just a hint of excitement
lingered…

Nathan and his friend
Nicholas Alexander
had traveled long and far
to visit Nicholas's cousin Henri.

Today, they were going
for a hot air balloon ride.

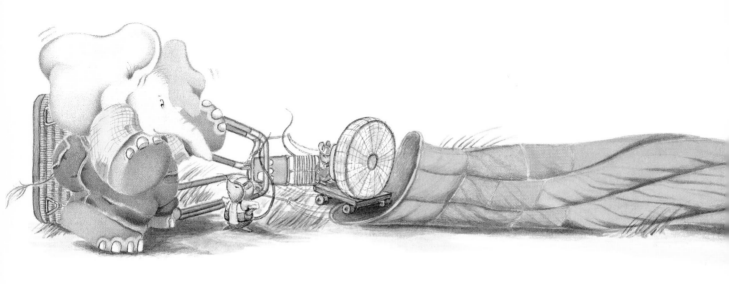

Nathan was impatient.
"I want to blow up the balloon, Cousin Henri,"
said Nathan. "May I? May I?"

"Don't call me cousin!
I'm Nicholas's cousin
and not yours.
And, to answer your question,
no, you may not blow up the balloon.
You are too young and too clumsy."

"You see, Nathan," explained Nicholas
when he saw his friend was a little hurt.
"It's no simple affair getting air
inside the balloon and heating it with fire."
"Fire?" asked Nathan.
"Yes. Hot air makes the balloon float.
It's lighter than cool air."
"Oh," said Nathan. "I see."

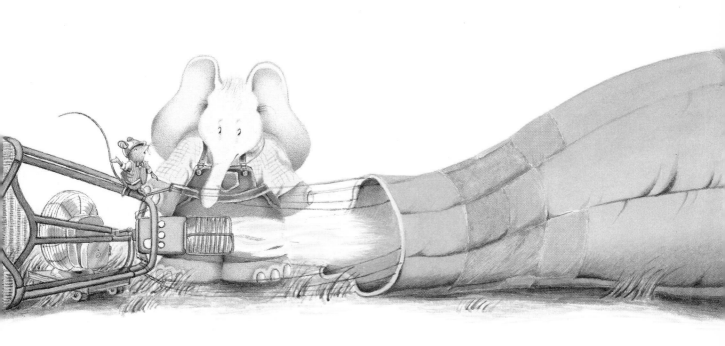

"Does he really have to come?"
whispered Henri.
"Nathan is my friend," said Nicholas.
"A friend, perhaps," said Henri,
"but too young, too big, and no help."

"Come, Nathan. We are ready!
Let's climb inside," said Nicholas.
"I can't wait! Let's fly! Let's fly!"
cried Nathan.
"Let's take off!" commanded Henri.
"Let's ride the winds!"

Airborne.

"Wow!" said Nathan, leaning over the basket.
"Look at those houses! They are just like toys!"
"Careful, Nathan," cried Henri.

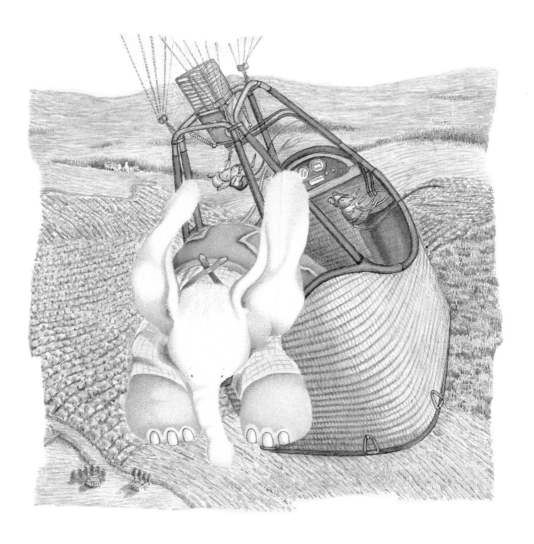

"You are tilting the ba-a-a-a-a-sket!!"

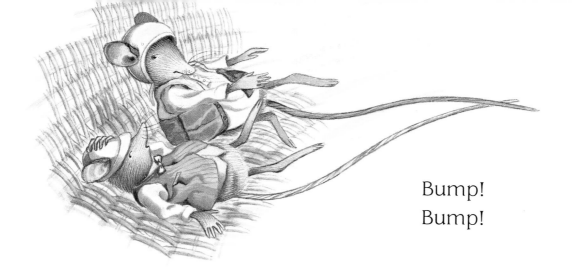

Bump!
Bump!

"You see, Nicholas?" said Henri.
"It was *your* bad idea to bring
him."

"No, Nathan!" cried Henri.
"Don't feed the birds!"

"Go away!"
Flap, flap, flap, flap!

"Ouch!"

"Oh, my!" cried Henri.
"We are running out of fuel."

"*Quick!* We must look for a
landing place."

"There!" said Nicholas.
"That farm!"

'Good choice!" said Henri. "But—
he wind is carrying us too fast!"

"We're heading toward the barn—"
said Nathan. "Oh!"

"We are going to crush the chickens!"

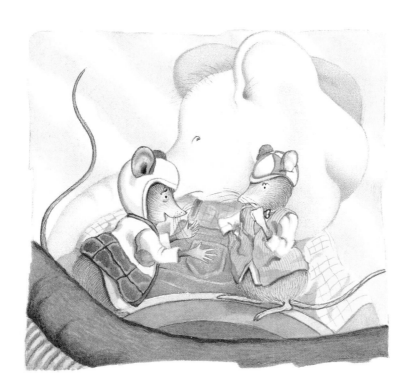

"We are all out of fuel," said Henri.
"I can't lift the balloon!"

"Oh, NO!!!" cried the farmer's wife.

"Crouch in the middle
of the basket!" commanded Henri.
"This will be a
horrendous landing!"

"Wait!" said Nathan.
"I can help!"

"You…?" said Henri.
"Try!" whispered Nicholas.

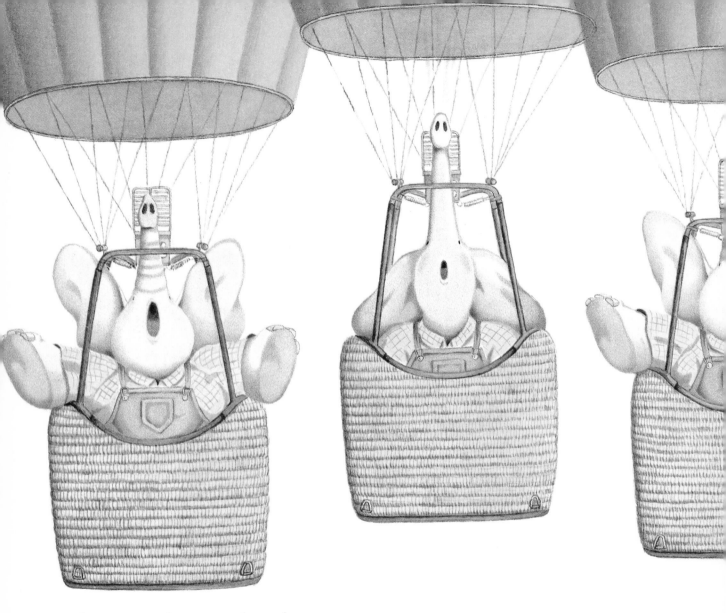

Nathan stood up and took one huge breath and exhaled it into the balloon.

Then he took two huge breaths and exhaled them into the balloon.

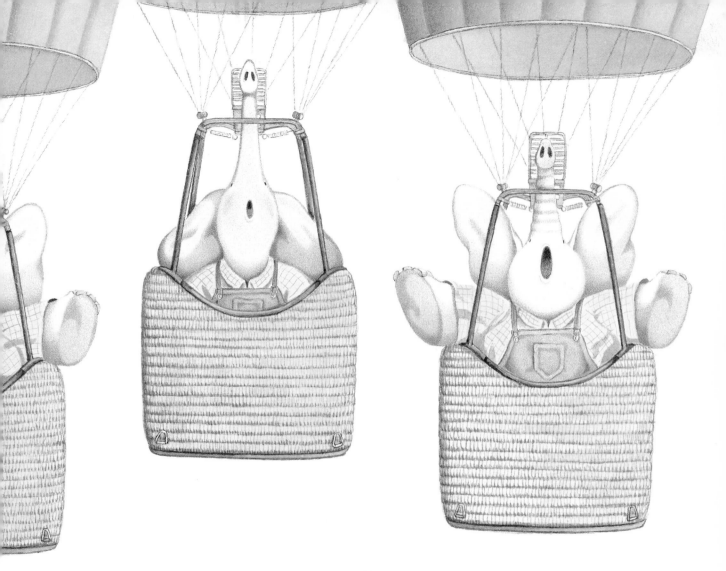

Finally he took three huge breaths
and exhaled them into the balloon.

Because Nathan had lifted
the balloon a bit,
Henri managed to land it farther away.
The chickens were safe!
And so were they.

Nathan was exhausted —
but radiant.
He had saved the day.

The farmer's wife was so happy
that she invited Nathan,
Nicholas, and Henri
to a hot bowl of pumpkin soup,
and a loaf of warm bread
with sweet butter.

"See, my dear Henri,"
said Nicholas,
"it was indeed a good idea
to bring Nathan."
"I must admit it was good,"
said Henri. "Even very good —
Oh! By the way, Nathan,
from now on, call me — if you please —
Cousin Henri."

Feeling full and content,
the three cousins took a
nap in the sun.

9